JACK, THE TURTLE WHO WANTED TO FLY

By Michael B. Cameron

Jack, the Turtle who wanted to Fly

Written by Michael B. Cameron
Illustrated by Nina Mkhoiani

To my Daughter, Katana,
I hope where ever you go, you choose to fly,
love Dad.

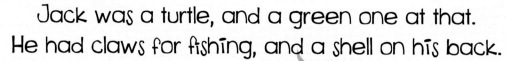

Jack was a turtle, and a green one at that.
He had claws for fishing, and a shell on his back.

He looked like any turtle, that you or I had seen.
But inside jack was different; inside Jack had a dream.

The other Turtles all said that he was mad
Turtles didn't fly, even if they wanted to, no matter how bad.
"Give up on flying", they said, "be happy in the pond".
But Jack kept on dreaming, He knew they were wrong.

So Jack left the pond and headed on up the hill
He Left the other turtles behind, laughing at him still

He had to go, he had to try.
There must be somebody on the hill, that could teach him to fly.

The first thing he met, was a bull frog named Jed
Jed didn't fly, he liked to jump instead.
Jump, Jump, Jump, went Jed with a thump.
The last thing Jack saw was Jed Jump over a stump.

Jumping looked neat, Jack thought to himself
But he wanted to fly, surely someone could help.

So on up the hill, went the turtle named jack,
Slowly but surely with a shell on his back

The next thing Jack met, was a snake named Jake,
He was fat in the middle, from something he ate.
He slithered and hissed and had a forked tongue
And was laying around, enjoying the sun.

"Hello Mr. Snake", said Jack. "I want to fly.
Can you teach me how? I sure want to try.
Jake rolled his eyes and looked up at Jack
Then he stooped hissing, and started to laugh.

The snake kept on laughing, so Jack went on his way
He'd find someone to help, and he'd find them today.

So on up the Hill, went the turtle named Jack.
Slowly but surely with his shell on his back.

Jack climbed over a log, and stopped dead in his tracks.
There was a baby bird and a big fat Rat!.
Now was the rat's chance to have a nice baby bird snack.
That bird needed help, and it was all up to Jack!

The rat moved forward, licking his lips.
Jack stood his ground, ready for nasty rat tricks.
The rat jumped forward, trying to bite our poor Jack.
But the rat didn't know about the hard shell on Jack's back!

Jack pulled in his head, then his legs and his arms.
Everything tucked in, out of reach, out of harm.
The rat bit and he clawed and he gnawed and he chewed

But Jack's shell was too hard;
that mean old rat just couldn't get through.

Suddenly there was a whoosh, and the rat looked around.
Then he ran off, because he knew that sound.
Jack peeked out his head, then his arms and his legs.
And there was the Mother Bird,
cawing over her just hatched egg.

"You saved my baby", said the Mother Bird to Jack
"Now I owe you a favor -- anything you want, go ahead just ask".

Jack said, "Well there is one thing, Can you teach me to fly?
I know I'm just a turtle, But I've come all this way and I sure want to try".

The mother bird smiled and said, "Turtles can't fly,
Turtles live in the Pond, not up in the Sky.
But you are special, she said, with a glint in her eye.
So I tell you what I will do, I will give you a ride.

She grabbed his shell and up, up they went.
Up in the sky, just like Jack had dreamt.

They flew through the clouds, they danced in the sky
And the other birds stared, saying, "Turtles can't fly".

The Mother Bird dropped him off, and he skimmed into the Pond
While the other turtles stared on, realizing they had been wrong.
"You flew Jack!, You flew! What was it like?"
"It was wonderful, just wonderful, I felt like a kite.

Now every night when it's dark and it's still,
The baby turtles gather, to hear about Jack's trip up the hill.

And every night he finishes with a grin in his eye.
You can do anything Jack says, all you have to do, is to try.

THE END

Made in the USA
Las Vegas, NV
02 November 2024

10871345R00017